Get That Pest!

Erin Douglas
Illustrated by Wong Herbert Yee

Green Light Readers
Harcourt, Inc.
Orlando Austin New York San Diego London

Mom and Pop Nash had ten red hens.
Every day they got ten eggs.

One morning, five eggs were missing!

“Someone has robbed our hens!”
shouted Pop.
“We can’t let him get another egg!”
said Mom.

The Nashes hid in the shed.

C-C-Crick. "What's that?" asked Mom.

A wolf slipped
into the shed.

He popped four
eggs into his sack.

"It's a wolf!" shouted Mom.
"I'll get him!" shouted Pop.

"Too bad," said Pop.
"Get this net off me!" shouted Mom.

Now only ONE egg was left.

“We have to get that pest!” said Mom.
“Help me set this trap,” said Pop.
When the trap was set, they hid.

C-C-Crick . . . Smash!

The trap got Mom and Pop.
The wolf got the last egg.

Then Mom and Pop Nash set a BIG trap and hid.

C-C-Crick . . . Womp!

"Let me out," begged the wolf.
"You can have all the eggs back."
"You didn't eat them?" asked Pop.

“No,” said the wolf. “I PAINTED them.”
“Oh my!” said Mom.
“Well, well,” said Pop.

Painted
Eggs

Now Mom and Pop Nash
sell painted eggs.
Would you like one?

ACTIVITY

The Missing Eggs Game

Play the missing eggs game.

WHAT YOU'LL NEED

white paper

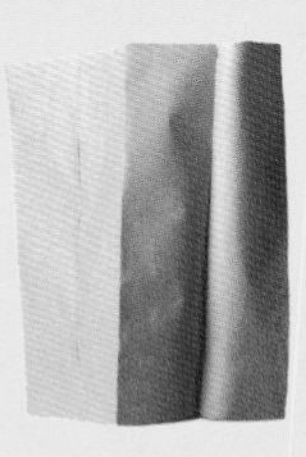

bag

scissors

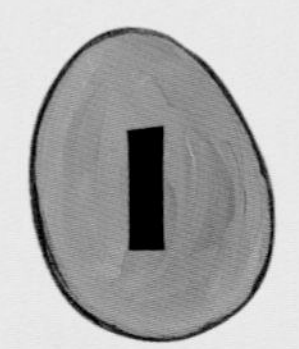

1 Cut out 6 eggs.

2 Lay them in a row.

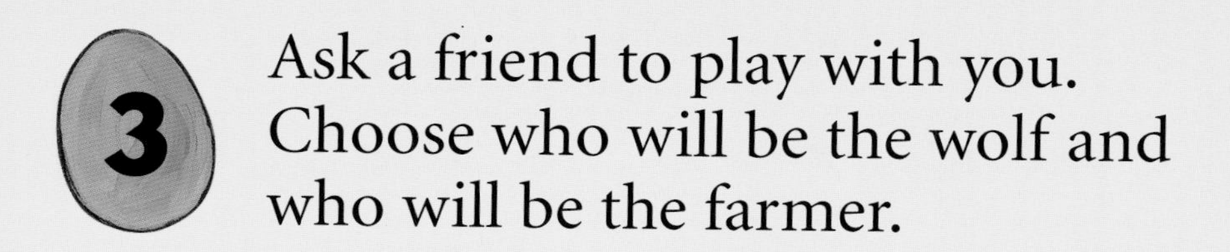

3. Ask a friend to play with you. Choose who will be the wolf and who will be the farmer.

4. When the farmer isn't looking, the wolf takes some of the eggs and puts them in a bag.

5. The farmer must tell the wolf how many eggs were taken.

6. Play again. Be sure to take turns being the wolf and the farmer!

Meet the Illustrator

Wong Herbert Yee always wanted to be an artist. He started writing and illustrating children's books when he was an adult. His daughter is his helper. She tells him if she thinks other children will enjoy his stories.

Wong Herbert Yee

For information about permission to reproduce selections from this book, please write Permissions, Houghton Mifflin Harcourt Publishing Company 215 Park Avenue South NY NY 10003.

www.hmhbooks.com

First Green Light Readers edition 2000

Green Light Readers is a registered trademark of Harcourt, Inc., registered in the United States of America and/or other jurisdictions.

The Library of Congress has cataloged an earlier edition as follows:
Douglas, Erin.
Get that pest!/Erin Douglas; illustrated by Wong Herbert Yee.
p. cm.
"Green Light Readers."
Summary: When a farmer and his wife discover that something is stealing the eggs laid by their ten red hens, they set up elaborate traps to catch the thief.
[1. Eggs—Fiction. 2. Farm life—Fiction. 3. Stealing—Fiction.]
I. Yee, Wong Herbert, ill. II. Title.
PZ7.D74643Ge 2000
[E]—dc21 99-6801
ISBN 978-0-15-204873-0
ISBN 978-0-15-204833-4 (pb)

SCP 10 9 8 7
4500368300

Ages 5–7
Grades: 1–2
Guided Reading Level: G–H
Reading Recovery Level: 14–15

"A must-have for any family with a beginning reader."—*Boston Sunday Herald*

"You can't go wrong with adding several copies of these terrific books to your beginning-to-read collection."—*School Library Journal*

"A winner for the beginner."—*Booklist*

Five Tips to Help Your Child Become a Great Reader

1. Get involved. Reading aloud to and with your child is just as important as encouraging your child to read independently.

2. Be curious. Ask questions about what your child is reading.

3. Make reading fun. Allow your child to pick books on subjects that interest her or him.

4. Words are everywhere—not just in books. Practice reading signs, packages, and cereal boxes with your child.

5. Set a good example. Make sure your child sees YOU reading.

Why Green Light Readers Is the Best Series for Your New Reader

- Created exclusively for beginning readers by some of the biggest and brightest names in children's books
- Reinforces the reading skills your child is learning in school
- Encourages children to read—and finish—books by themselves
- Offers extra enrichment through fun, age-appropriate activities unique to each story
- Incorporates characteristics of the Reading Recovery program used by educators
- Developed with Harcourt School Publishers and credentialed educational consultants